Mac Side Up

WORDS AND PICTURES BY BOB ELSDALE

DUTTON CHILDREN'S BOOKS · NEW YORK

Copyright © 2000 by Bob Elsdale

All rights reserved.

CIP Data is available.

Published in the United States by Dutton Children's Books,

a division of Penguin Putnam Books for Young Readers

345 Hudson Street, New York, New York 10014

www.penguinputnam.com

Designed by Ellen M. Lucaire

Printed in Hong Kong

First Edition

1 2 3 4 5 6 7 8 9 10

THIS BOOK IS DEDICATED TO **MY MOTHER**.
WITH THANKS TO **MICHAEL WALLIS**, FOR HIS IDEAS AND ENTHUSIASM;
MY WIFE, **CHRISTINE**, AND MY TWO CHILDREN, **HOLLY** AND **ROBBIE**,
FOR THEIR LOVE AND SUPPORT;
AND TO **JOAN POWERS** AT DUTTON CHILDREN'S BOOKS,
FOR MAKING THIS BOOK HAPPEN.

Mac was one cool cat. Sure, he was handsome, clever, and brave. All cats are. But Mac was something more. He loved adventure.

Dusty was one cool ferret. When Dusty and Mac played hide-and-seek, Dusty found all the best places to hide. Cereal boxes were a favorite, especially the ones with free gifts inside. On this day, she'd found a pair of pink glasses.

Dusty peeked out of the box and *whoosh!* Mac pounced. He surfed across the table on a slice of warm, buttered toast.

The toast fell down, down, and *plop!* It landed butter-side down on the floor.

Mac landed on his paws.

As he cleaned up the floor with his rough tongue, Mac wondered, *Why does toast always land the wrong way up, but cats always land the right way up? . . . Hmmmm.*

Later, as he lay in bed, Mac kept thinking about that toast. Then he had a strange thought. *What if . . . what if I strapped a piece of buttered toast to my back and jumped from a great height? What would happen?* Mac wasn't sure, but he knew he had to find out.

In the morning, Mac had a plan. Dusty ferreted around in the desk and found paper and markers. Mac drew a picture of how he would solve the mystery. He drew a special truck and himself.

Dusty added a pile of mattresses. She knew, of course, that cats have nine lives. She wasn't sure how many lives Mac had already used up, but she knew it was always a good idea to be careful.

There was a vehicle that would be perfect for the stunt. It was made from an old ice-cream truck joined with a fire engine. They sold ice cream from the front and used the back for bungee-jumping.

Dusty checked the equipment while Mac looked on. "You'll need a crash helmet, too," she told Mac.

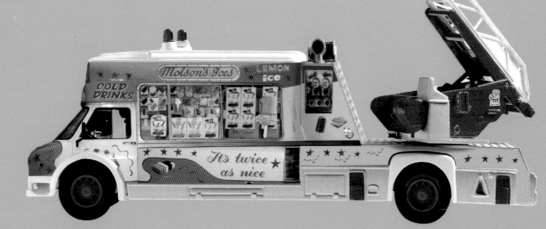

The big day arrived. A crowd of people gathered to see what was going on. Once everything was ready, Mac was slowly pulled up. Higher and higher he went. Dusty had fitted a walkie-talkie to Mac's helmet so she could talk to him from ground control.

The countdown began.

FIVE

It certainly is high up here, thought Mac.

FOUR

Yes, very high.

THREE

Remember, cats are clever, thought Mac.

TWO

Mac shut his eyes and took a big breath.

Remember, cats are brave . . .

Dusty pulled the lever, and Mac hurtled toward Earth. He shouted into his microphone: "This is cool! This is a breeze!"

Dusty wished she had thought about a parachute. And what was that seagull doing there?

The seagull had spotted the toast, and he was hungry. He tried to spear it. But Dusty had superglued the toast to the plate. The seagull tried again, but his shiny beak slid off the slippery plate and put Mac in a spin. The world was upside down!

Would Mac and the toast land right-side up? Or butter-side down?

But Mac, like all cats,
was clever—and brave.
And he was one cool cat.

He started to straighten. He was almost the right way up. Could he do it?

YES!

A perfect landing.
One giant leap for catkind!

PURRFECT LANDING??

Mac the cat took one of his nine lives into his own paws this morning when he conducted an experiment designed to determine whether buttered toast, when dropped, ~~will~~ always land butter-side down.
...ers at several major universities
...lications of this experiment.
...ly stolen by a seagull

The crowd cheered. Mac and Dusty gave high fives. Mac had done it. He had proved that cats always land on their paws—and toast does not always land butter-side down.

Mac's picture was in the paper. His great leap was shown on TV. He was even given a gold medal.

FOR A VERY BRAVE AND SPECIAL CAT it said on the back.

It was true.

The cat used in the production of this book is a professional cat model. He has starred in a number of TV commercials and is accustomed to being photographed.

   Dusty is a family pet and was perfectly happy showing off in front of the camera.

   At no time was either Mac or Dusty hurt or distressed in any way during the production of these photographs.

                                                    —BOB ELSDALE

The pictures in this book were all created by using computers to combine lots of individual photographs. Some of them contain up to fifty different parts. This gives you an idea of how it was done.